Macbeth

#killingit

more omg shakespeare!

srsly Hamlet
YOLO Juliet
A Midsummer Night #nofilter

Macbeth

#killingit

william shakespeare

+

courtney carbone

Random House New York

For all the slackers being quizzed on this tomorrow 📝,
good luck. 🍀
—C.B.C.

Text copyright © 2016 by Penguin Random House LLC

Emoji copyright © Apple Inc.

Image on page 4 copyright © Shutterstock/Nejron Photo, page 18 copyright ©
Shutterstock/IvanKravtsov, page 25 copyright © Shutterstock/Syda Productions, page 27
copyright © iStock/HutchinsonVisuals, page 46 copyright © Shutterstock/2xSamara.com,
page 55 copyright © Shutterstock/Africa Studio, page 70 copyright © Shutterstock/BMJ,
baby page 75 copyright © Shutterstock/Gelpi JM, pregnant woman page 75 copyright ©
Shutterstock/MariyaL, page 77 copyright © Shutterstock/Gelpi JM

Visit us on the Web! randomhouseteens.com

Educators and librarians, for a variety of teaching tools,
visit us at RHTeachersLibrarians.com

Library of Congress Cataloging-in-Publication Data
Carbone, Courtney.
Macbeth #killingit / William Shakespeare and Courtney Carbone.
pages cm
Summary: "William Shakespeare's tragedy told in the style of texts,
tweets, and status posts"—Provided by publisher.
ISBN 978-0-553-53880-9 (trade) — ISBN 978-0-553-53881-6 (ebook)
[1. Shakespeare, William, 1564–1616. Macbeth—Adaptations.] I. Shakespeare, William,
1564–1616. Macbeth. II. Title. III. Title: Macbeth hashtag killingit. IV. Title: Macbeth #killing it.
PZ7.C1863Mac 2016 [Fic]—dc23 2015008606

MANUFACTURED IN CHINA
10 9 8 7 6 5 4 3 2 1
First Edition

who's who

 Macbeth, Thane of Glamis and co-commander of Duncan's army

 Lady Macbeth

 Duncan, king of Scotland

 Malcolm, Duncan's older son

 Donalbain, Duncan's younger son

 Banquo, co-commander of Duncan's army and Macbeth's friend

 Fleance, Banquo's son

 The Three Witches

 Hecate, goddess of witchcraft

 Macduff, a Scottish noble

 Lady Macduff

Macduff's Son

Send

who's who (cont.)

💼 Seyton, Macbeth's servant

💀💀💀 The Three Murderers

😷 Doctor

👒 Gentlewoman

🔑 Porter

🎩 Lennox, a Scottish noble

🎩 Ross, a Scottish noble

🎩 Angus, a Scottish noble

🎩 Menteith, a Scottish noble

🎩 Caithness, a Scottish noble

🏴󠁧󠁢󠁥󠁮󠁧󠁿 Siward, commander of the English soldiers

👦 Young Siward, Siward's son

💂 Captain in Duncan's army

‼️ Apparitions: an Armed Head, a Bloody Child,
a Crowned Child, and eight nonspeaking kings

💼💼💼 The Three Servants

characters you won't meet in this book
(aka people w/o smartphones)

 An Old Man

A Doctor at the English court

A Soldier

 Attendants, Servants, Lords, Thanes, Soldiers
(all nonspeaking)

Send

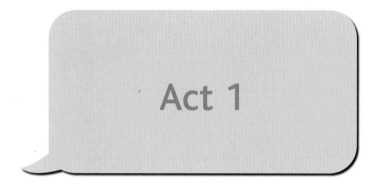

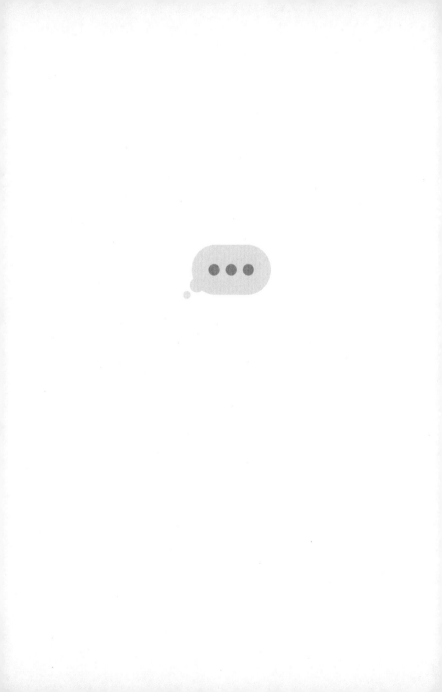

[Scene 1]

Group text: The Three Witches

witch #1

When do u witches wanna meet up next? In thunder 💥, in lightning ⚡, or in rain 🌧️?

witch #2

When the hurly-burly's done. ❗ 🌀 🔥 When the battle's lost 👎 and won 👍.

witch #3

Right b4 the setting sun. 🌇

witch #1

Location TBD?

witch #2

Upon the heath. 🏞️

witch #3

There we'll find Macbeth. *heh heh*

witch #1

G2g. My 🐱 needs kibble!

Send

witch #2

And my 🐸 needs his .

witch #3

Kk I'll b here.

witch #1

😃 = 😔 and 😔 = 😃 #WitchesBCrazy

[Scene 2]

Captain has posted a new picture to album:
The Battle for Scotland #BattleSelfie

👍   REPLY

Duncan: What's up w/ the battle, Captain? 💥
The pics 👀 pretty intense—you must have
been rite in the middle of everything! 👍

Send

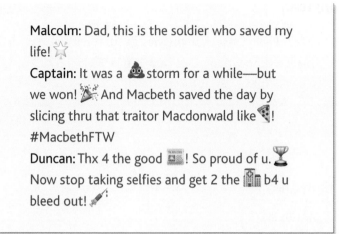

Group text: Duncan, Ross, Malcolm

DUNCAN

What's going on, Ross? How's my favorite Thane?

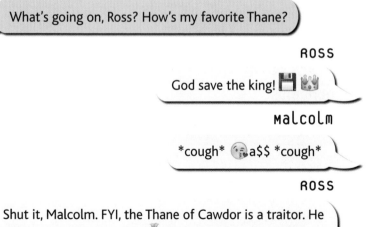

ROSS

God save the king! 💾 👑

MALCOLM

cough 😘a$$ *cough*

ROSS

Shut it, Malcolm. FYI, the Thane of Cawdor is a traitor. He sold us out to the enemy 💰, but we caught him, NBD.

Send

Duncan

WTF?! Really? 😠 That guy was great at parties. Guess the only thing 2 do now is take away his title and give it to ... wait for it ...

ROSS

ME

Duncan

ROSS

*MACBETH #AutocorrectFail 😳

Malcolm

Ha, riiight. 😉

Duncan

Macbeth sure chose a good day 2 b a hero. 💥

Send

[Scene 3]

🧒 Witch #1
It's 🎉⏰! Where my girls @?

👍   REPLY

Witch #2: Oh, you know, killing 🐷 🐷 🐷.
Witch #3: U?
Witch #1: Well, I won't bore u w/ the details, but there was a 👫 and a ⛵ and some 🌰s. She didn't want to share, 🐽. Let's just say, it didn't end well for her. LMAO.
Witch #3: I 👂 a drum! Macbeth is almost here. U guys remember the chant?
Witch #1: We weird sisters 🧒 🧒 🧒...
Witch #2: 🤚 in 🤚, travel all over the 🌍...
Witch #3: 💃 💃 💃, 3 + 3 + 3 = 9. Yay! The spell is ready. 🔮

Macbeth

Banquo, I'm almost there. This weather is TERRIBLE!! ⚡🌂 At least we won! Did you 👀 I'm #Trending?! ✅

Send

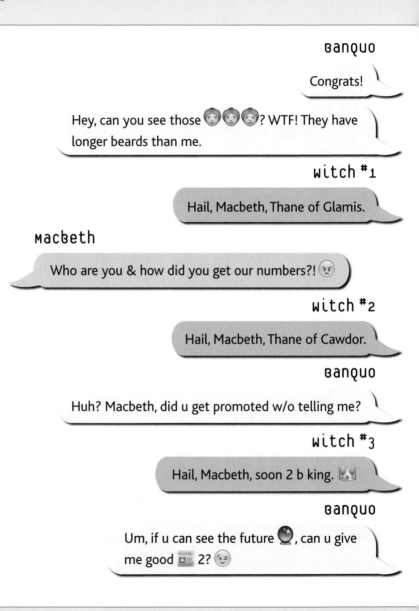

witch #1

Banquo, < lesser than Macbeth and greater >.

witch #2

Not as happy 😄, but much happier 😉.

witch #3

You'll have 👑s, but you won't be 👑 yourself.

All hail Macbeth & Banquo! 🙌

Macbeth

Huh? I'm Thane of Glamis already. But IDK anything about Cawdor. Last I heard, that guy was still alive. (And the life of every party! 🎉) And 👑? Well, that's just crazy 🌀🌀! Tell me more . . . ?

Not Delivered

Banquo

Hello??

Not Delivered

Banquo

Hey, Macbeth, my txts to 🧙🧙🧙 aren't goin thru. 😫

Send

Macbeth

They prob heard you comment on their beards. 👏 #SlowClap #TypicalBanquo

Sux 2 be u, man. All those royal 👶s, but never 👑 urself?

Banquo

Ha, right. Like ur actually gonna be 👑! 😊

Group text: Ross, Angus, Macbeth, Banquo

Ross

Hey. I know ur still OTW 🏠 from battle, but just FYI the king is pretty 😃 w/ u, Macbeth.

Angus

And . . .

Ross

He chose u as the new Thane of Cawdor. 🍀

Macbeth

But the old Thane of Cawdor's still alive . . . rite? I don't wear borrowed kilts, if u know what I mean. #ThaneLife

Send

ROSS

Yeah, he's alive, but 😵 to the 👑. He admitted to treason and everything. It's all you. 💰💰💰

Macbeth

Wow, thx! 😎

Macbeth

Banquo, I'm Thane of Cawdor! Do you think this means your 👶s will be 👑 after all?

Banquo

They said u were gonna be 👑 remember?! But we should b careful. Maybe it's all a trick. 🎃

Macbeth

Yeah, the best trick EVER! 👍

Send

Banquo

Can the 😈 tell the truth?

🧹 The Three Witches like this.

[REPLY]

[BACK] **MACBETH** [+]

Okay. Let's look @ the facts. 📊 The Cawdor thing is great 📰 , but I can't become 👑 , can I? Not until Duncan dies, anyway. And IMHO I don't 👀 that happening any ⏰ soon.

To-Do List:

1. Patiently wait for Duncan 2 die 😵

2. Become king of Scotland when old & feeble 👴

3. Cry about my wasted life 😭

PS: Unless Duncan invites himself to my 🏰 , my wife and an imaginary 🗡 convince me 2 stab him, I blame it on some servants 👬 , his heirs mysteriously disappear, etc. etc. Like THAT would ever happen! I feel guilty just thinking about it. My 💜 is racing.

#WishfulThinking

Send

Macbeth looks kinda weird rite now. His hair is standing up & I can literally 👂 his 🖤 pounding. Gonna keep my 👀 on him. #Creeper

[Scene 4]

Duncan

Hey, son, has the old Thane of Cawdor been "taken care of" yet? 🗡

Malcolm

Yep, I've gotten 📩 that Cawdor is officially 😵.

Duncan

About ⏰! How'd it go?

Send

malcolm

He was surprisingly brave. 😵 Prob the most impressive thing he ever did in life was die lol. 😵 ⭐ 👏 (Too soon??)

Duncan

I still can't believe it. I rly trusted that guy! Never shoulda bought those matching BFF kilts . . .

Group text: Duncan, Macbeth, Banquo

Duncan

Congrats and thx, Macbeth. You've given me more than I could ever repay. 🗡️

macbeth

Just having ur 👍 is enough, D. 😃

Duncan

Still, I'll 👀 out for you from now on 💰💰💰 & Banquo 2 💰.

Banquo

U gave us the chance to succeed! #Blessed

Send

ɒuncan

Speaking of succeed—I have an announcement 2 make. Brb.

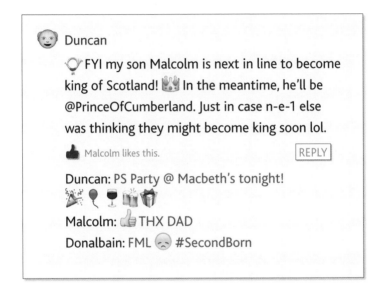

Duncan

🔮 FYI my son Malcolm is next in line to become king of Scotland! 👑 In the meantime, he'll be @PrinceOfCumberland. Just in case n-e-1 else was thinking they might become king soon lol.

👍 Malcolm likes this.   REPLY

Duncan: PS Party @ Macbeth's tonight!
🎉 🎈 🍷 🎁 🎁

Malcolm: 👍 THX DAD

Donalbain: FML 😞 #SecondBorn

Malcolm

🎵 Oh, I just can't wait to be . . . sued for copyright infringement. 🎵 😏

👍   REPLY

Send

UGH! MALCOLM is Prince of Cumberland now? Well, that sux. It's gonna be a lot harder to become 👑. #AlwaysTheThane 😔
Hmm, I gotta keep these 😈 💭s & my black 🖤 out of the 🔦.
Long 📖 short, I need to look 😇!

[Scene 5]

📬 Welcome, Lady Macbeth! You've got 2 new messages marked "Urgent."

❗ Macbeth	Oh, NBD, just Glamis, Cawdor, and soon-to-be KING
❗ Duncan	Party tonight @ Inverness! All ages! No cover!

Send

BACK **LADY MACBETH** +

OMG?! Me, queen of Scotland?? Better start trying on crowns! 👑💁 But Macbeth can be such a 🍼. He's 2 nice to speed up the process, if u know what I mean. 😉 I'll have 2 do some convincing. . . .

Come, 👻👻👻, and change me from a 🚺 to a 🚹. Fill me from head 2 👠 with cruelty. #SorryNotSorry

📥 Lady Macbeth has added 📕 *How to Kill Friends and Influence Peasants* to cart.

☑️ Macbeth has just checked into Inverness Castle.

👍 Lady Macbeth likes this.

Lady Macbeth

> Bae! Such awesome 📰! U r going to be KING 👑! 😘

Macbeth

> About that . . . u heard Duncan is coming here <u>tonight</u>?

Send

Lady Macbeth

Yes. When is he leaving?

Macbeth

Tomorrow.

Lady Macbeth

Don't worry. I will make all "the plans" for Duncan. *wink wink* Just act natural, look 😇 but be a 🐍.

[Scene 6]

✅ Duncan has checked into Inverness Castle—with 15 others.

👍 Lady Macbeth likes this.

Duncan

I love ur 🏰! This is gonna b the best trip ever!

Lady Macbeth

Of course! My 🏰 is your 🏰. We're thrilled you could come.

Send

[Scene 7]

Okay. So now the king is IN my 🏰. It's almost like he WANTS me 2 kill him. 🙁 My wife is pressuring me, but 🗡ing a 👑 is kinda a big deal. I gotta make a 📋 of pros & cons.

Reasons NOT 2 Kill Duncan: 🌸 🌈 ☀

1. He is a guest in my 🏡.
2. What goes around comes around. 🔄
3. He just gave me, like, one billion presents. 🎁🎁🎁🎁🎁🎁🎁🎁🎁🎁🎁🎁
4. Everyone 💚 him and will be super depressed. 😔
5. Killing another human is TERRIFYING. 😱

Reasons 2 Kill Duncan: 💰 🏰 👑

1. Ambition ✓
2. Umm . . .

Send

Lady Macbeth

Where r u? Why did u leave the 🎉?

Macbeth

Are ppl 👀 4 me?

Lady Macbeth

Obvi! Ur the HOST!!!

Macbeth

FYI it's not happening.

Lady Macbeth

What's not happening?

Macbeth

U know what. Duncan just gave me a big 🏆 and every1 keeps liking my statuses. I'm not throwing it all away so quickly.

Lady Macbeth

WTF is wrong with you?!?! Do you want 2b the 👑 or not?!

Send

Macbeth

Babe. STOP. ✋

Lady Macbeth

😒 SMH, u said b4 that u'd do it if u had the chance 🎲, but now u actually have the chance 🎲 & ur too SCARED?! That's bull 💩.

Macbeth

U don't understand.

Lady Macbeth

I don't understand?! 😠 You PROMISED me! I know what it's like to 🖤 & 🍼 a 👶, and I would literally murder my own 👶 if I PROMISED to.

Macbeth

Umm ... okayyy.

Lady Macbeth

NBD I'm just trying 2 get my point across.

Macbeth

What if it doesn't work?

Send

Lady Macbeth

LMAO! Just screw 🍗 up ur courage & it will work. We'll frame his servants 👬: give them drugs 💊 and alcohol 🍹, wait for them to pass out 😴, and cover them in Duncan's blood. Piece of 🍰!

Macbeth

Will ppl believe it? 🙁

Lady Macbeth

ROTFLMAO! Of course! What else would ppl think? We'll b crying hysterically 💦😭😭💦 the whole ⏰!

Macbeth

Fine. I'll do it. Now go pretend to b a good hostess while I figure out how 2 avoid getting caught. Ttyl.

Lady Macbeth

Kk, might wanna start by deleting these txts. . . . 😉

Macbeth Reminders

2 items   Edit

☐   Don't have kids w/ Lady Macbeth

☐   Delete incriminating texts

Send

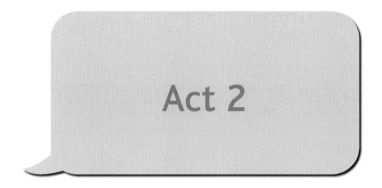
Act 2

[Scene 1]

Macbeth

Hey, Banquo! What's going on?

Banquo

Oh, hey! I thought you'd be 😴 by now. The king is passed out. Congrats on throwing the 🎉 of the year. 😃 Duncan was making it ☔! #SWAG 🎁🎁🎁

Macbeth

Anything good?

Banquo

Lolz ur 👰 got an ENORMOUS 💎.

Macbeth

Dammit. Never gonna hear the end of that.

Banquo

Heh.

Um, I had a dream last nite about those 3 witches 👵👵👵. Weird the Cawdor thing came true . . .

Send

Macbeth

I COMPLETELY 4got about that. 😇 We can talk it over when we have more ⏰.

Banquo

What? 😦 U forgot they said u'd become Thane of Cawdor like a half hour b4 u became Thane of Cawdor?

Macbeth

Heh, yeah. 😬 Welp, ⏰ 4 ᶻzᶻ. Catch up later?

Banquo

K. 😞

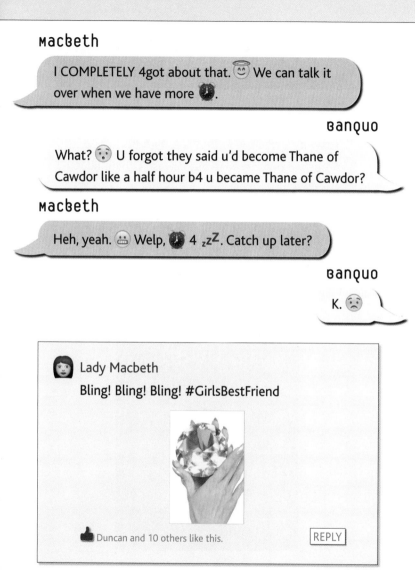

👩 Lady Macbeth

Bling! Bling! Bling! #GirlsBestFriend

👍 Duncan and 10 others like this.

REPLY

Send

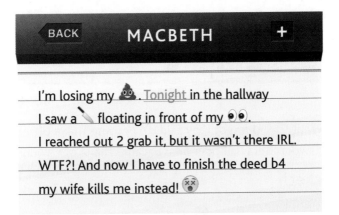

I'm losing my 💩. <u>Tonight</u> in the hallway
I saw a 🔪 floating in front of my 👀.
I reached out 2 grab it, but it wasn't there IRL.
WTF?! And now I have to finish the deed b4
my wife kills me instead! 😵

🎵 Macbeth is listening to Metallica's "Enter Sandman"

Send

[Scene 2]

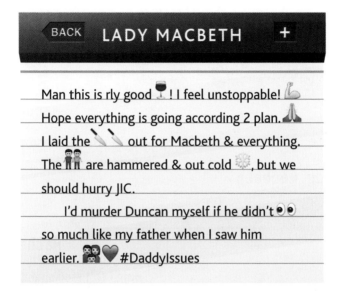

LADY MACBETH

Man this is rly good 🍷! I feel unstoppable! 💪
Hope everything is going according 2 plan. 🙏
I laid the 🔪🔪 out for Macbeth & everything.
The 👬 are hammered & out cold ❄️, but we
should hurry JIC.

I'd murder Duncan myself if he didn't 👀
so much like my father when I saw him
earlier. 👨‍👧 🤍 #DaddyIssues

Lady Macbeth

> Where r u?

Macbeth

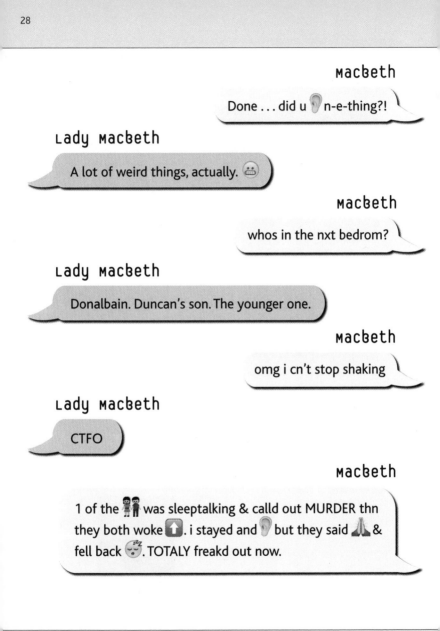

Lady Macbeth

Pull urself 2gether. I can barely understand u!!

Macbeth

😫 the 👫 cried out "God bless us!" & *Amen." but I couldn't say Amen 🙏 the words got stck in my throat!!! Y DID THT HAPPEN?!

Lady Macbeth

U can't worry about that right now. You'll go crazy. 🌀🌀

Macbeth

An then some1 yelled 😴🚫. Macbeth has 🗡️zzᶻ. Macbeth will 😴 no more!

Lady Macbeth

What? Wait, that pic u just sent. Was that the murder weapon? Why do u still have those?! Go 🗡️ your 👁️👁️. & put those bloody 🗡️🗡️ back on the 👫!!! We have 2 stick 2 the plan! 📋

Macbeth

i can't go bck there! I can brely type! Autocorrect has forsaken me. Just like Heaven!

Send

Lady Macbeth

Srsly, u r acting like a 👶! Bring them 2 me & I'll do it myself. FML.

Macbeth

All the 👣 in the 🏔 could not wash this blood off my 🫱. I 👂 knocking on the 🚪. some1 is comin to get me!

Lady Macbeth

I put the 🔪 on the 👫. My 🫱 r bloody 2 but you don't c me 😭. I'm off 2 🛁. Put on your pjs in case some1 👀 u.

Macbeth

that knockin is loud enough to wake up 😵 Duncan!

🎵 Macbeth is listening to Justin Bieber's "Bad Day"

Send

[Scene 3]

✅ Macduff and Lennox have checked into Inverness Castle.

🔑 **Porter**

I may as well be the 🚪keeper to 🔥😈🔥 w/ all this knockin. If I wuz the 😈's 🚪keeper, i'd hafta use my 🔑 to 🔒🔒🔒🔓 the 🚪 all day longggg. . . .

👍   [REPLY]

Macduff: Must have been a good 🎉. This place 🍺 of 🍻.

Porter: Heh, u know wut happens wen u drink? 🍻🍷🍸

Macduff: What's that?

Porter: 1) it makes ur 👃 red, 2) makes u z$_z$Z & 3) hafta 🚽.

Macduff: The more you know 🌈 . . .

Porter: that's not all! it makes u wanna 💏 but instead u end up limp 🍆. 👩

Macduff: Lol, you speak from experience? 😉

Community Manager: ⚠️THIS POST HAS BEEN FLAGGED FOR OBSCENE CONTENT. ⚠️

Send

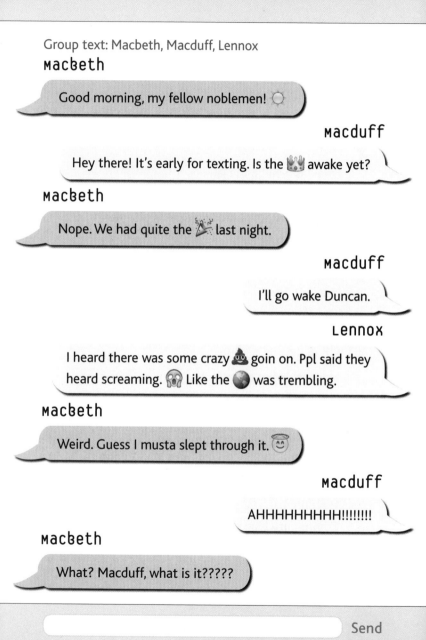

Lennox

Did something happen to the 👑?

Macduff

Meet me up here and 👀 for yourself!!! 🙈🙉🙊

🧑 Macduff

🚨 Ring the alarm 🔔! The 👑 has been murdered! Treason! 🗡️💀🗡️ Ring the 🔔!!!!! 🚨

👍 | REPLY |

Lady Macbeth: 💁‍♀️💁‍♀️💁‍♀️ In our 🏠???

Banquo: Who cares where it happened?

Macbeth: If I died an hour ago, I would have had the perfect life. ☀️🖼️ But now, everything will be terrible 4ever. 💀 The meaning of life has been poured out like a 🍷.

Donalbain: What's up?

Macbeth: ICYMI the 🎂 of ur blood has stopped. 😫

Macduff: Your father 👑 was 🗡️💀. OMG I can't believe it.

Malcolm: Oh. Who do u think did it?

Lennox: 👉👬. The servants and their 🗡️🗡️ are covered in blood. It's a blood 🛁.

Send

Macbeth

Macbeth has added "Vigilante Justice" to his list of interests.

👍 Lady Macbeth likes this. | REPLY |

Banquo: WHAT DID YOU DO? 🙈🙈🙈
Macbeth: FYI I just killed the 👩‍👦. That 👆? 😞
Macduff: *facepalm* Why would you do that, Macbeth?! Now we'll never know what happened!
Macbeth: Who can be 😀😔🙄😐😤 all at once?? Duncan was MURDERED. Who wouldn't avenge his death on social media?! 👊

Lady Macbeth

OMG OMG OMG I'm going to pass outttttttttttttttttttttttttttttttttttttttttjbjkbjkb

👍 | REPLY |

malcolm

> D, why aren't we saying anything 😶 when we're the king's sons? 👨‍👨‍👦 👑 💚

Donalbain

> ⚠️ We have to be careful, bro. The killer might come 4 us next. There are 🔪🔪 in their 😀s. And next in line = motive. Let's GTFO of here. There will b plenty of ⏰ 2 😭.

malcolm

> Tru. And ⏰ 4 us to get revenge. 😡

● ● ●

🧔 **Banquo**
Everyone, get dressed. 👔 👖 👗 We'll regroup in a few to see if we can figure out what happened.

👍   REPLY

Macduff: 👍
Macbeth: Meet ⬇️ stairs in 10.

Send

Malcolm and Donalbain have checked out of Inverness Castle. #OffTheGrid

 Macbeth likes this.

[Scene 4]

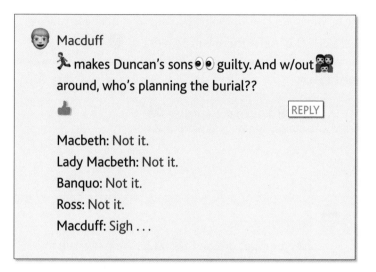

 Macduff

🏃 makes Duncan's sons 👁👁 guilty. And w/out 👩‍👩‍👦 around, who's planning the burial??

👍   REPLY

Macbeth: Not it.
Lady Macbeth: Not it.
Banquo: Not it.
Ross: Not it.
Macduff: Sigh . . .

Send

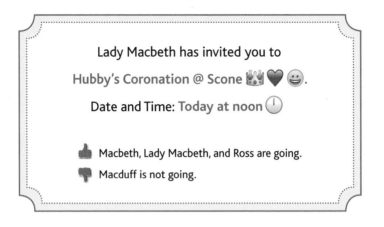

Lady Macbeth has invited you to

Hubby's Coronation @ Scone 👑🖤😃.

Date and Time: Today at noon 🕛

👍 Macbeth, Lady Macbeth, and Ross are going.

👎 Macduff is not going.

Macduff has invited you to

King Duncan's Burial ⛪🐝😭.

Date and Time: Today at noon 🕛

👍 No one has yet responded.

Send

Act 3

[Scene 1]

✅ Malcolm has checked into England. 🇬🇧

✅ Donalbain has checked into Ireland. 🍀

← BACK   **BANQUO**   **+**

Duncan is 😵. I still can't believe it. Today
Macbeth was named the new 👑, just as the
👩👩👩 predicted. 🔮 Something's 🐟🐟.

● ● ●

Macbeth

Banquo! We could have used you @ my 👑ing today.

Banquo

Ah, sorry. 🙁 I was out riding. 🐴

Macbeth

Np. But don't miss dinner tonight!

Send

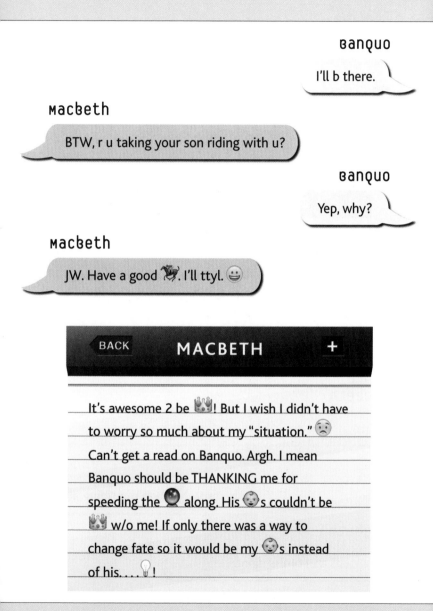

👑 KINGSLIST 👑

Wanted: 2–3 Able-Bodied Men (Inverness)

- Do you want to make more 💰?
- Is your life 💩?
- Want to get back at those who have wronged you? 👊
- Okay with morally ambiguous objectives? 😉
- Know how to wield a 🔪? 💀

If you answered yes to any of these questions, stop by the castle today!

REPLY

Principals only. Recruiters, please don't contact this job poster.
Do NOT contact us with unsolicited services or offers.
Posted by Macbeth

[Scene 2]

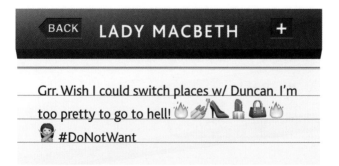

BACK **LADY MACBETH** +

Grr. Wish I could switch places w/ Duncan. I'm too pretty to go to hell! 🔥 💅 👠 💄 👜 🔥
🙍 #DoNotWant

Send

Lady Macbeth

Macbeth, where have u been? R u still obsessing about the murder? What's done is done. 🎵❄️ Let it go! ❄️🎵 It's 🍴⏰.

Macbeth

How can I eat when Banquo and Fleance are still alive?!

Lady Macbeth

IDK. But we'll all die eventually! 💀

Macbeth

Just brace urself. It's gonna b a bumpy ride. 📶

Lady Macbeth

What's THAT supposed 2 mean?

Macbeth

I could tell you . . . but then I'd have to kill you. 😉

Lady Macbeth

Lol, OK. I'll wait and 👀👀.

Send

[Scene 3]

Group text: The Three Murderers

murderer #3

> You the other guys from the Kingslist ad?

murderer #1

> Who the 🔥😈🔥 gave u our #s?

murderer #3

> Macbeth, obvi. He gave me all the details. 🧔🏇🔪

murderer #2

> *shrug* He must b legit if he 👃 the murder plans. 📋

murderer #1

> Fine. It's ⏰. Hide and 👀 for Banquo and Fleance.

murderer #3

> Do you hear that? 🐎🐎

murderer #2

> I see a 🔦!!

Send

murderer #3

💩💩💩 OMG the kid got away!

murderer #2

1 outta 2 ain't bad? 😆

murderer #1

We gotta find Macbeth. He's not gonna be 😄.

[Scene 4]

✅ Macbeth, Lady Macbeth, Ross, and Lennox have checked into "Macbeth's First Annual Kingsgiving!"

> 👦 Macbeth
> 🏆 Hello, royal subjects! Find your seats so we can get started. 🍴 Our table is so long we set up a chat room to talk. #FirstWorldProblems
> 👍   REPLY
>
> Lady Macbeth: Don't forget to use #Kingsgiving

murderer #1

Hey, boss, I need 2 talk 2 u asap.

Send

murderer #1

macbeth

Now just tell me you killed Fleance 🙏, and I will be the 😎 👑 in all the 🌍.

murderer #1

👎

macbeth

💩

SMH. Well, that's TERRIBLE news. But at least Banquo is 😵. I can deal with Fleance l8r. 😈

● ● ●

Lady macbeth

Get in here ASAP. We're all sitting around the table waiting 4 you. 😠

macbeth

Kk one sec, babe. Dealing with something over here.

Send

#Kingsgiving Chat Room

Macbeth: It looks like everyone has checked in except for Banquo. Hopefully he's just 🏃 late, and not in any kind of ⚠️! Did anyone save me a seat? #Kingsgiving

Lennox: Of course! Right at the head of the table. 🍗🍽️🍷 #Kingsgiving

Banquo's ghost has checked into "Macbeth's First Annual #Kingsgiving!"

BANQUO'S GHOST: YEAH, MACBETH. I GOT YOUR SEAT RIGHT HERE. 😠 #KINGSGIVING

Macbeth: Holy 💩! Who's messing with me?! #Kingsgiving

Lennox: Huh? WTF. #Kingsgiving

Ross: What's going on? 🙁 #Kingsgiving

Macbeth: You can't say I did it. Leave me alone!!! 👻 #Kingsgiving

Lennox: Did what? Ruin a perfectly good 🎉? Lolz #Kingsgiving

Ross: Do you guys wanna reschedule? 📅 It seems Macbeth is a little under the weather ☔ . . . or something. . . . #Kingsgiving

Lady Macbeth: Oh, don't mind him. 😊 He gets like that sometimes. Please start eating 🍽️🍴 and he'll be back to his old self in no ⏰. #Kingsgiving

Banquo's ghost has checked out of "Macbeth's First Annual #Kingsgiving!"

Send

Lady Macbeth

What's WRONG with you!? Pull it together!

Macbeth

Didn't you see that post in the #Kingsgiving feed from Banquo??? 😬 ICYMI he's taunting me! 👻

Lady Macbeth

What are you talking about!? 🌀🌀 There was no post from Banquo! It was just Lennox, Ross, and all the other lords. You're acting like a 🫣!

Banquo

Yeah, Macbeth. You're just hallucinating. None of this is real. 👻

Macbeth

It's still happening! Even now! Can't you see it?

Lady Macbeth

No idea what ur talking abt. Restore ur 📱 to factory settings. AND ACT NORMAL! 😠

Send

Banquo

Yeah. Just act normal, Macbeth. Lol.

Macbeth

STOP! 🚫 Why are u doing this, Banquo?! 😰

Lady Macbeth

Stop it! Macbeth, ur acting crazy. And I look like an @$$ 4 texting in the middle of dinner! 👁 🍴

Macbeth

He's come 4 me, 2 avenge his death. I'm sure of it. That's how these things go. I should have known. 😧

Lady Macbeth

Look. We still have guests here. 🍺 🍷 Take a minute, pull urself 2gether, and come back to the dining room.

Send

#Kingsgiving (Cont.)

Macbeth: Sry 4 being a creepy weirdo. I'm all good now. Just get a little 🌀🌀 from time to time. #Kingsgiving

Banquo's ghost has checked into "Macbeth's First Annual #Kingsgiving!"

Macbeth: STOP IT! LEAVE ME ALONE! #Kingsgiving

Lady Macbeth: Oh, lol. Here we go again! Someone cut him off! 🎁 💁 #Kingsgiving

Macbeth: If you were a 🐻 or 🦏 or 🐯, then maybe u could scare me. But you're 🚫. You're just a 👻! #Kingsgiving

Banquo's ghost has checked out of "Macbeth's First Annual #Kingsgiving!"

Ross: 🙁 Wuts wrong, Macbeth? #Kingsgiving

Lady Macbeth: U know what, I think Ross's ⚖️ ✅ idea is probably 4 the best. Why don't u all grab a 🍽️ & take it 🏡 w/ u? #Kingsgiving #2Go

Lennox: Sure thing. Feel better, M! 👋 #Kingsgiving #WhatJustHappened

---

👦 Macbeth

"Macbeth's First Annual #Kingsgiving!" has been canceled.

👍   REPLY

Send

Lady Macbeth

> Well, I hope ur 😃.

Macbeth

> Blood will have blood. 💉 That's what they say, isn't it? Hey, whatever happened to Macduff?

Lady Macbeth

> Did he RSVP?

Macbeth

> No, but I 👂 he was coming 2 town. I have spies 👥 all over the kingdom now, just in 💼. 😏

> I g2g see the 🔮🔮🔮 & figure out a 📋 of action. There's no turning back now. #InIt2WinIt

[Scene 5]

Group text: Hecate, The Three Witches

Hecate

> Well, I hope u witches r proud of urselves. 👏 Giving Macbeth 🔮s w/o asking me 1st. 😠

Send

witch #1

Boss, you seem 😠.

Hecate

You think?! From now on, u all need 2 do as I 👄.
Meet with Macbeth again, but this ⏰ do it rite. Got it?

witch #1

👍

witch #2

👍

witch #3

👍

[Scene 6]

🧑 Macduff
Just chillin' with my new BFF, king of England. 🇬🇧

👍   REPLY

King of England: #TeamMacduff #TheOneTrueKing

👍 Lennox likes this.

Send

Act 4

[Scene 1]

📍 **The Three Witches have created a new Kingterest board.**

Spell for Macbeth

Group Text: The Three Witches

witch #1

U witches ready?

witch #2

2x, 2x, toil & 🎼.

witch #3

TrOUble, not trEble.

witch #2

Same diff.

Send

● ● ●

📍 Macbeth has saved "Spell for Macbeth" board to favorites.

Group text: The Three Witches

witch #2

> Ugh. 👀 out. Something 😈 this way comes. #Macbeth

witch #1

> Txt him b4 he starts uploading selfies & ruins the whole board!!

Group text: The Three Witches, Macbeth

witch #3

> What do u want, Macbeth?

macbeth

> What up, witches? 😎

witch #1

> Wouldn't u like 2 know.

Send

Macbeth

K now I see a child wearing a 👑 and carrying a 🌳 branch! I don't get it. It says "Macbeth shall not lose power 'til Great Birnam Wood comes 2 Dunsinane."

Witch #3

We know, Macbeth. We sent them 2 u.

Macbeth

So what's the catch? A 🌳🌳🌳 can't move, right? So . . . I will be 👑 4ever!

Witch #1

U said it, not me.

Macbeth

This is v helpful, but I have 1 last ❓. Y will Banquo's 👶s be 👑 but mine won't? 😔

Witch #1

No spoilers!

Macbeth

I'll curse u if u don't tell me. 😡

Send

witch #1

Fine, but don't say we didn't warn u. . . .

👶👑👶👑🧔👶👑👶👑👶👑👶👑
👶👑👶👑🔮 #PurposefullyVague

Banquo FTW.

macbeth

Starting 2 think there's more 2 this than u guys are letting on. . . . ⚠

Not Delivered

Hello? ⚠

Not Delivered

📍 Macbeth has added 5 new selfies to "Spell for Macbeth" board.

● ● ●

lennox

Macbeth, FYI Macduff has gone to 🇬🇧.

macbeth

WTF. He must b out 2 get me! The only reasonable thing 2 do now is 🔪 Macduff's whole 👨‍👩‍👧.

Send

Lennox

> That feels ... extreme. Is your 👑 on too tight?

[Scene 2]

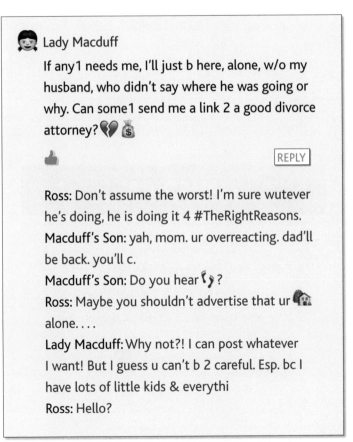

👧 Lady Macduff

If any1 needs me, I'll just b here, alone, w/o my husband, who didn't say where he was going or why. Can some1 send me a link 2 a good divorce attorney? 💔 💰

👍   REPLY

Ross: Don't assume the worst! I'm sure wutever he's doing, he is doing it 4 #TheRightReasons.

Macduff's Son: yah, mom. ur overreacting. dad'll be back. you'll c.

Macduff's Son: Do you hear 👣 ?

Ross: Maybe you shouldn't advertise that ur 🏠 alone. . . .

Lady Macduff: Why not?! I can post whatever I want! But I guess u can't b 2 careful. Esp. bc I have lots of little kids & everythi

Ross: Hello?

Macbeth Reminders

3 items   Edit

☐   Don't have kids w/ Lady Macbeth

☐   Delete incriminating texts

☑   Hire ppl 2 kill Macduff's wife & kids

[Scene 3]

📥 Malcolm has added 📕 *Trust Issues for Dummies* to cart.

◄ BACK   **MACDUFF**   ＋

To-Do List:

1. Get on Malcolm's good side. 😇
2. Convince him to attack Macbeth. 👊
3. Hire repairman 👶🔧🐀 to fix broken 🔒 on front 🚪.
4. Check in with wife and kids. 👨‍👩‍👧

Send

malcolm

Macduff, aren't u worried abt leaving ur wife & kids alone 2 fend 4 themselves?

macduff

Instead of answering that perfectly good ❓, I'm just gonna say I would NEVER do what Macbeth has done. Not for all the 💰 👑 🏰 in the 🌍.

malcolm

ICYMI 🇬🇧 is sending 10,000 troops 2 fight Macbeth. 👊 Since I'm supposed 2 b 👑, now wud prob b a good ⏰ 2 mention that I'm not xactly the most upstanding person, ya know? Next to me, Macbeth looks pure as ❄️ ⛄ ❄️.

macduff

WTF? Macbeth is worse than the 😈 himself.

malcolm

Yeah, but I kinda got a thing 4 the ladies. 💃 💃 💃 If I was 👑, I'd just 🔀 all the time. And not in a cute bf/gf way. 👫 Know what I mean? 😉

Is there a bed emoji? That could help get my point across. 😉

Send

macduff

No, I'm good. Listen, ur Duncan's heir! U can't be worse than Macbeth!!! Just keep it in ur 👖 in public, & 💋 on ur own ⏰.

malcolm

K, well, there is sumthing else.

macduff

facepalm Go on . . .

malcolm

I'd probably steal all the 💎 💎 💎 and 🏠🏠🏠 in the kingdom. #AllTheThings

macduff

Look, Malcolm. We can get u plenty of 💎 💎 💎 and 🏠🏠🏠 when ur 👑. NBD.

malcolm

Yeah, & that'd prob b enough if I wasn't THE WORST HUMAN BEING THAT EVER LIVED.

macduff

💩 I give up. Ur unfit 2 be 👑.

Send

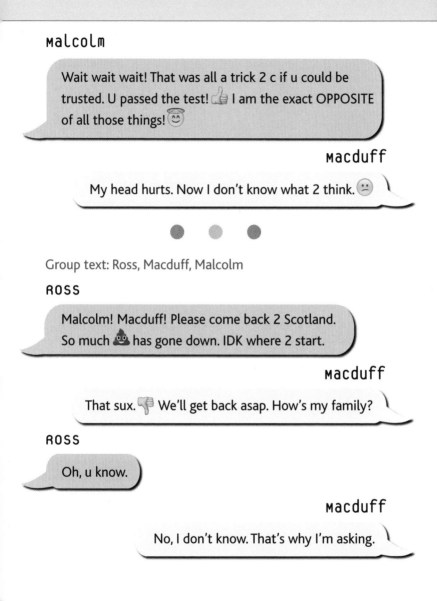

ROSS

They r fine . . .

ish.

macduff

What does that mean? TELL ME

ROSS

They're all dead. 😵 👨‍👩‍👧

macduff

NOOOOOOOOOOOOOOOOOOOOOOOOOOOOOOOOO

OOOOOOOOOOOOOOOOOOOOOOOOOOOOOOOOOO

OOOOOOOOOOOOOOOOOOOOOOOOOOOOOOOOOO

ROSS

Yeah, if u knew how bad it was u'd probably drop 😵 from shock. Sorry 2 b the 🐻er of bad 📰.

Send

macduff

Why did I leave them alone?! *facepalm* FML

malcolm

This has Macbeth written all over it. We need 2 take that guy out NOW. 👊

macduff

Macbeth doesn't have any children. So I can never get even. But I'll do what I can 2 get revenge. 😡

malcolm

Good timing. The 💂💂💂💂💂 from 🇬🇧 should be ready by now. Let's go kick a$$! 💥

Send

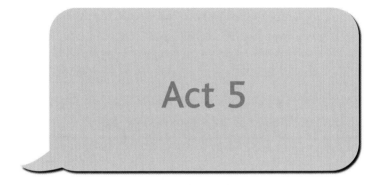
Act 5

[Scene 1]

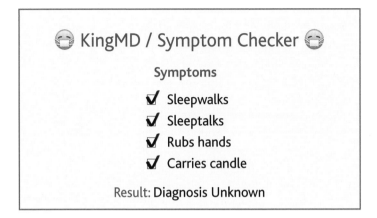

😷 KingMD / Symptom Checker 😷

Symptoms

☑ Sleepwalks
☑ Sleeptalks
☑ Rubs hands
☑ Carries candle

Result: **Diagnosis Unknown**

gentlewoman

Doctor, we desperately need ur help! Lady Macbeth is ᶻᶻᶻwalking, ᶻᶻᶻtalking, carrying around a candle, and rubbing her hands together like a madwoman. 🌀🌀

Doctor

I see. And what kinds of things is she saying?

gentlewoman

Things like "Out, damned spot!" 🧟 & "Who would have thought the 👴 had so much blood in him?" & "The thane of Fife had a 👰," etc. 😨👹

Send

Doctor

It 👂 to me like she needs an 🎩 more than a 😷! Keep your 👀 on her, and make sure she doesn't get her 🖐 on anything dangerous. 🗡💣💉

Gentlewoman

K, but I was kinda hoping for medical advice!! 😷

Doctor

IDK what to tell you.

Try bloodletting?

[Scene 2]

✅ Lennox, Angus, Menteith, and Caithness have checked into Great Birnam Wood.

👍 Macduff, Malcolm, and Siward like this.

Send

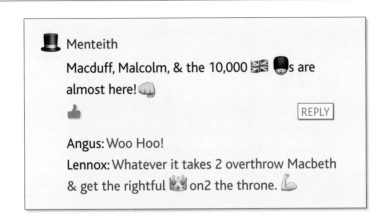

🎩 Menteith

Macduff, Malcolm, & the 10,000 🇬🇧 💂s are almost here! 👊

👍   REPLY

Angus: Woo Hoo!
Lennox: Whatever it takes 2 overthrow Macbeth & get the rightful 👑 on2 the throne. 💪

[Scene 3]

🧑 Macbeth

Man, I'd b rly nervous right now if it wasn't 4 those prophecies! 🔮 😃

👍   REPLY

Servant: Sir, u might wanna look out ur window. 🙈
Macbeth: Oh yeah? Well u might want 2 STFU!!!
Seyton: No, srsly, 💂💂💂💂💂 r coming 2 kill u.
Macbeth: Anyone else want 2 give me bad news?
Doctor: Your wife has gone crazy.
Doctor: Also I just sent you my bill. 📟
Macbeth: There it is. 😔

Send

[Scene 4]

Malcolm
Every1 break off 🌿s from 🌳s in Great Birnam Wood. We'll hide behind them 2 disguise ourselves. #DunsinaneOrBust

👍   REPLY

Siward: Ur ⌛ is ⬆️, Macbeth, or I'm not the commander of the 🇬🇧 💂s.
Malcolm: And he's totally the commander of the 🇬🇧 💂s, soooo ur ⌛ is ⬆️!
Siward: Thx for that totally unnecessary post, Malcolm.

[Scene 5]

Macbeth

Are we ready? Are all the soldiers in place? (The ones that haven't deserted.)

seyton

⚠️ IDK how 2 tell u this, but I have bad 📰. The queen is dead.

Send

Macbeth

FML. I guess she would have 😵 eventually. Every 17 turns in2 the next and there is nothing we can do 2 stop ⌛. Poof! 💨 Like a short-lived candle 🕯. Life is just a walking 🚶 shadow 👤, like 🎭 onstage, reciting memorized lines that sound important @ the time, but ultimately have 🚫 meaning.

seyton

TL;DR

Macbeth

Life sux & then u die.

seyton

True. 😔

● ● ●

servant

I know this sounds 🔘🔘, but it looks like Great Birnam Wood 🌳🌳🌳 is marching 2ward the 🏯!

Macbeth

WHAAAAT! OMG NO!!!!! It can't b true!!! 👖 🔥

Send

servant

> See 4 urself!

macbeth

> 💩

✅ Great Birnam Wood has checked into Dunsinane.

👍 The Three Witches like this.

[Scene 6]

🏂 Malcolm

Every1 throw ur 〚Y〛s on2 the ground! Blow the 🎺 🎺 🎺 !!! This one's for you, Dad!

👍 Siward likes this. [REPLY]

Siward: 💩 IS GOIN ⬇️ !

Send

[Scene 7]

Macbeth

Macbeth has created an online survey:

Were you born of a woman?

Start!

👍   REPLY

Young Siward

Young Siward scored 100%: Definitely born of a woman!

👍   REPLY

Young Siward: I was born of a woman, but I'm gonna fight you like a man.
Macbeth: *Wipes blood off sword* Nice try. Anyone else?

Send

[Scene 8]

macduff

> Face me, u coward.

macbeth

> Macduff? *sigh* I've already killed ur whole 👨‍👩‍👧. Isn't that enough?

macduff

> My 🗡 is my voice. #NoWords

macbeth

> Save urself the trouble. I'm 🍀 and can't be killed by any1 born of a woman, including u.

macduff

> Is that so?

Send

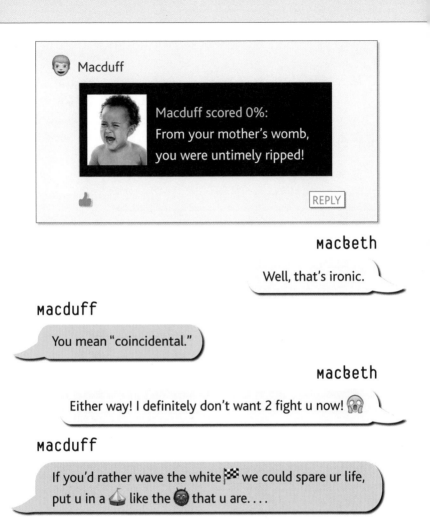

Macduff

Macduff scored 0%:
From your mother's womb,
you were untimely ripped!

REPLY

Macbeth

Well, that's ironic.

Macduff

You mean "coincidental."

Macbeth

Either way! I definitely don't want 2 fight u now! 😱

Macduff

If you'd rather wave the white 🏁 we could spare ur life,
put u in a ⛵ like the 🎃 that u are. . . .

Send

macbeth

Meh. That doesn't sound much better than dying a painful death. 🗡️💣💀

macduff

Meet me downstairs. Bring ur sword & let the games begin.

Group text: Malcolm, Siward, Ross

malcolm

I wish no one had 2 die. I hate how war has 2 be so violent. 🗡️💣💀✌️☀️🌈

siward

Life, ya know? But fortunately we didn't lose 2 many 🔼.

ROSS

Yeah, but we did lose ur son.

siward

😫 Tell me, were his wounds on his back (from 🏃 away) or his front (from 👊 valiantly)?

Send

ROSS

His front. 👍

siward

Well, that's all I can ask 4. I'm as proud as any father can be. 2 ☕☕☕ he goes. Hold on. I just got a txt from Macduff. . . .

👤 Macduff **has posted a photo to the album:**
NSFL Macbeth's Head on a Stick

👍 REPLY

Group text: Macduff, Malcolm, Ross, Siward

macduff

We won!!!! 🎉 Did you guys see what I just "posted"?? Get it?! #SeeWhatIDidThere

malcolm

YESSS!! 🎉

Send

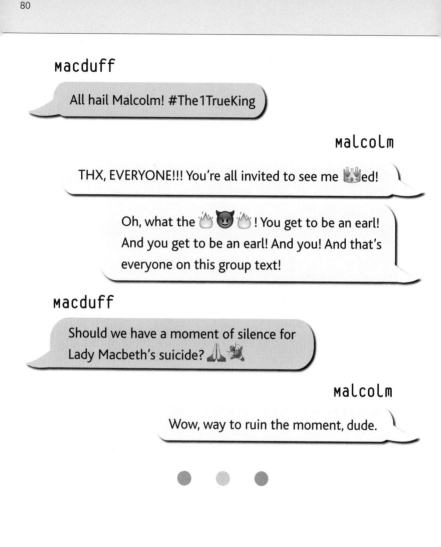

macduff

Hey, Malcolm, now that you're the king . . .
you were JK about all that stuff u said earlier:
🥷💎🏠😈, right? 😣

malcolm

Guess u'll just hafta wait & see. 😏

Send

The 411 for Those Not in the Know

411: Information

AKA: Also Known As

ASAP: As Soon As Possible

BFF: Best Friend Forever

BRB: Be Right Back

BTW: By The Way

CTFO: Chill The F*ck Out

FML: F*ck My Life

FOMO: Fear Of Missing Out

FTW: For The Win

FYI: For Your Information

G2G: Got To Go

GTFO: Get The F*ck Out

ICYMI: In Case You Missed It

IDK: I Don't Know

IMHO: In My Humble Opinion

IRL: In Real Life

Send

JIC: Just In Case

JK: Just Kidding

JW: Just Wondering

LMAO: Laughing My A$$ Off

LOL: Laughing Out Loud

LOLZ: Laughing Out Loud (ironically)

NBD: No Big Deal

NP: No Problem

NSFL: Not Safe For Life

OMG: Oh My God

OTW: On The Way

ROTFLMAO: Rolling On The Floor Laughing My A$$ Off

SMH: Shaking My Head

STFU: Shut The F*ck Up

TBD: To Be Determined

TL;DR: Too Long; Didn't Read

TTYL: Talk To You Later

WTF: What The F*ck?

WTG: Way To Go

YOLO: You Only Live Once

Send

some emotions you might find in this book

😠 Angry

😣 Anguished

😅 Anxious

😖 Confounded

🙁 Confused

😎 Cool

😵 Dead (or Dying)

😞 Disappointed

😳 Embarrassed (and/or Drunk)

😈 Evil (Devil)

😘 Flirty

😉 Friendly (wink, wink)

😤 Fuming Mad

😜 Goofy

😄 Happy

Send

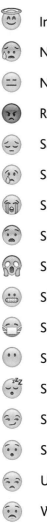

Innocent

Nervous

Nothing

Really Angry

Sad

Sad (and Crying)

Sad (and Sobbing)

Scared

Scared (and Screaming)

Sheepish (and/or Grimacing)

Sick

Silent

Sleepy

Sly

Surprised

Unamused

Worried

Send

COURTNEY CARBONE studied English and creative writing in Baltimore, before moving to New York City to become a full-time children's book editor. When she isn't collaborating with the greatest playwright of all time, Courtney can be found studying various forms of comedy and trying to finish the joke "Two groundlings walk into a bard. . . ." 👯‍♀️

@CBCarbone
CourtneyCarbone.com

WILLIAM SHAKESPEARE was born in Stratford-upon-Avon in 1564. He was an English poet, playwright, and actor, widely regarded as the greatest writer in the English language and the world's preeminent dramatist. His plays have been translated into every major language and are performed more often than those of any other playwright. 🎭

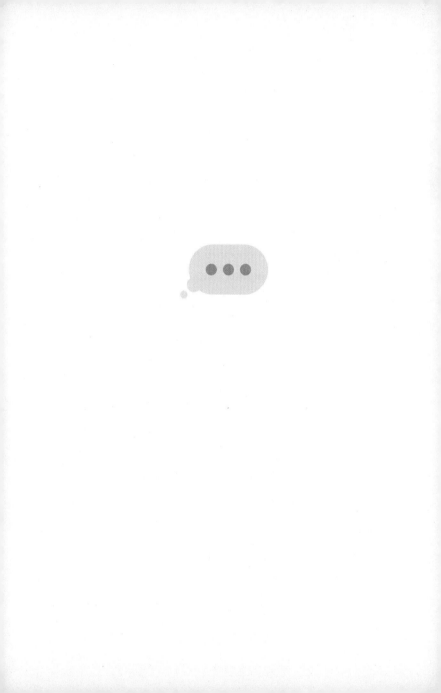

FOMO?

Read on for a peek at

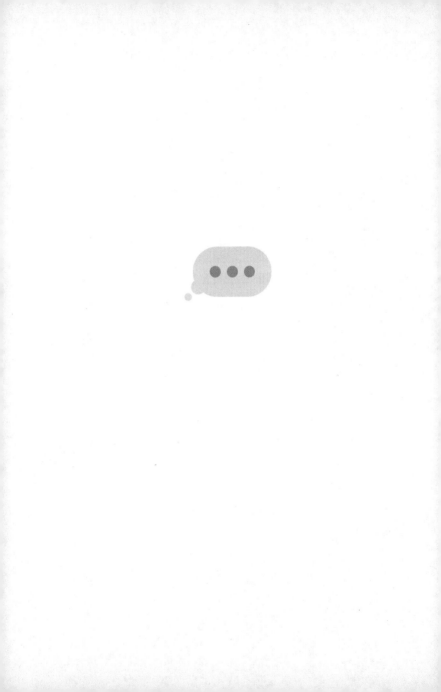

[Scene 1]

oberon

Soooo . . . wanna explain what's going on? 😡

That new 👦 from India should be one of my knights, not hanging out with you.

τιταηια

I can't even with you. ✌️

oberon

Excuse me. 🤚 As my wife, you're supposed to, IDK, listen to me!

τιταηια

You're pulling the MARRIAGE card? 😂 OK, then! Maybe you'd like to explain why you're sooo in 💚 with Hippolyta. You keep leaving our 🏠 to woo her, and everyone knows it.

oberon

HDU. Also, you're such a hypocrite. As if you aren't completely into Theseus. Psh. You've sabotaged all his relationships because of it. 💣 💥 🔥

Send

Titania

IDK. Maybe until after Theseus's marriage. 📅17

The fairies and I are celebrating <u>tonight</u>. 👯 I guess you can come if you get over yourself. Otherwise, leave us alone and we'll do the same for you.

oberon

Hand over the 👦 and I'll party with you. 🎉

Titania

BYE. 😠

● ● ●

oberon

Puck! Hey, ol' buddy, ol' pal. How's it going? 😄

Puck

Dandy! What's up?

oberon

I was just thinking 💬 ... and I remembered something. One night 🌙 I saw Cupid aim his bow and shoot an arrow 🏹 at a girl, but she was too busy to notice and I watched the arrow fall and hit a 🌼.

Send

oberon

> I kinda sorta maybe definitely need that 🏵 now. I showed it to you once. Remember?

puck

> Okeydoke, but why?

oberon

> Because, tbh, if you rub it onto someone's 👀 while they're 😴, then when they wake up, they'll fall in 😍 with the first person they see.

> Bring it to me quickly, please.

puck

> Aye-aye, captain. 👍

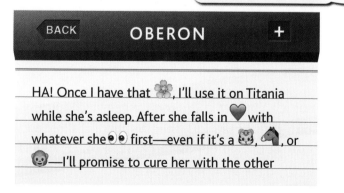

BACK · **OBERON** · +

HA! Once I have that 🏵, I'll use it on Titania while she's asleep. After she falls in 💚 with whatever she 👀 first—even if it's a 🐯, 🐴, or 🐵—I'll promise to cure her with the other

Send

plant 🌱 that I have—only if she agrees to let me have the 👦. Easy, breezy. Nothing can go wrong!

✅ Puck has checked into a flower garden in the forest.

● ● ●

✅ Demetrius has checked into the forest.

✅ Helena has checked into two trees behind Demetrius.

Demetrius

Are you following me ‼️⁉️👀

Helena

uhhh

💬

Demetrius

I see you behind that 🌳.

You have GOT to stop stalking me.

Send

nmf. i'm so crazy about u. u hold this power over me! ⚡🖤⚡

i can't let go until u let go of me.

Demetrius

WTF. 😠 I tell you constantly that I. Don't. Love. You. Never have, never will. Is that #closure enough?

Helena

😨 💔 if it wasn't for me, u wouldn't even know about hermia and lysander running away. so yw.

Demetrius

And I've been going in 🌀🌀 trying to find them. Were you really lying? Was this a trick to be alone with me?

Helena

no, i swear! i'm like ur little 🐶. i'm always going to follow u around. it's kinda cute, y/y? 🐾

Demetrius

Ugh, you make me 😷.

You shouldn't be here, you know, all alone in the woods.

Send

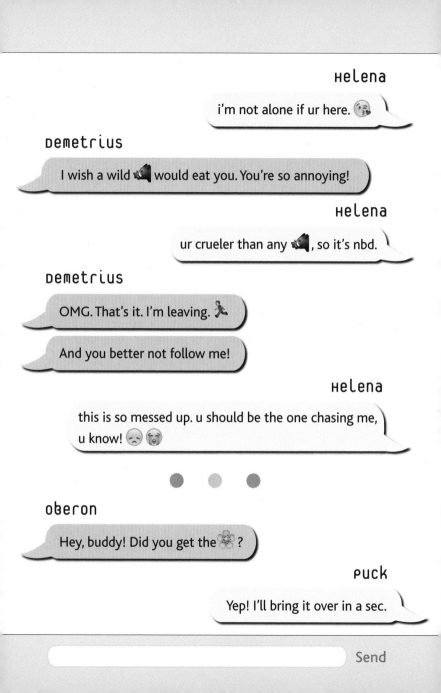

oberon

Awesome! I want you to keep some of it as well.

I'm going to find Titania. But with your part, I need you to do me a favor.

I overheard a couple fighting in the forest just now. Can you perform a little switcheroo? 😏 Find the man from Athens, and make sure you rub a huge amount of the 💮 on his 👀. He'll be chasing her for once, hehehe. 😈 TTYL!

[Scene 2]

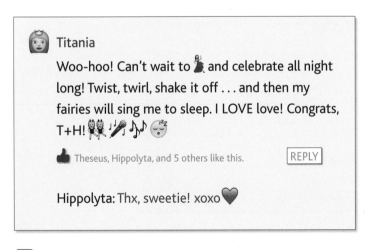

👸 Titania

Woo-hoo! Can't wait to 💃 and celebrate all night long! Twist, twirl, shake it off . . . and then my fairies will sing me to sleep. I LOVE love! Congrats, T+H! 👯 🎤 🎶 😴

👍 Theseus, Hippolyta, and 5 others like this.   REPLY

Hippolyta: Thx, sweetie! xoxo 🖤

✅ Oberon has checked into Titania's chambers.

Send

Great—she's asleep. $_z$z^Z Now to squeeze this 🌼 into her 👀. When you wake up, you'll love whatever you see first. Even if it's a 🐮🐸🐭🐘. TT4N.

● ● ●

✅ Lysander and Hermia have checked into a part of the forest they swear they've seen before.

✅ Lysander has checked into a grassy knoll.

✅ Hermia has checked into a cozy bush a few trees away from Lysander.

Lysander

> Hey, what are you doing all the way over there? 🙁

Hermia

> IDK. Maybe we shouldn't sleep so close together. 🎩

Lysander

> Sorry! I wasn't trying to get fresh with you—promise. 😈

Send

Lysander

I just think it would be nice to finally be close to each other. The whole night. ⭐🌙

Two 🖤🖤, one sweet spot.

Hermia

Ooh, you flirt. I'm almost convinced.

But it's better this way. 😘 We have to be good until we're married. 💍

Lysander

Amen. 🙏 Sweet dreams!

> 😍 Lysander
> Can't find my way out of Athens, but at least I get to sleep next to my bae. 😘 —feeling lost 🌀
> 👍 REPLY

● ● ●

✅ Puck has checked into the forest.

Send

I've been running around this forest all day and I haven't seen anyone from Athens! 🏃👟😄 I'm exhausted. 👀 Aha! A couple sleeping. So this must be the guy who doesn't love this girl. I know what to do. 🌸 Hope this makes you fall in love with her so hard that you'll never sleep again. 😍🖤

● ● ●

✅ Demetrius has checked into a different part of the forest.

HELENA

> can u plz slow down?? i can't keep up w/u.

✅ Helena has checked into four trees behind Demetrius.

DEMETRIUS

> 🏃🌲🌳🌲

> You're more attached to me than my own shadow! Get a clue. 🔍 I'm trying to lose you.

Send

Helena

fine. leave me here in the dark. idc n-e-more.

Demetrius

Great! Bye!! 👋

> Helena
>
> life is a bottomless pit. ⚫ i'll never be good enuf for him—feeling bummed. 😔
>
> 👍 Helena and two others like this.   REPLY

● ● ●

✅ Helena has checked into the grassy brush.

Helena

🌲👀🌲

lysander, is that u? u awake?

Lysander

YAWN. I was just resting my eyes.

Wait. 👀

Send

Helena, is that you over there? 😨

How have I never noticed before? You're so beautiful! You're as bright as the ☀ today!

Is Demetrius with you? I could kill him for the way he treats you! 🔪

Helena

y? it doesn't matter. he luvs hermia, but she luvs u.

u don't have n-e-thing to worry about. ur lucky. 🍀 be happy w/hermia.

Lysander

Happy with Hermia ‼ Yeah right. 👎

She is capital B booorrring. I don't even like her, let alone love her.

In fact, I love YOU, Helena! 😍 💋

Send

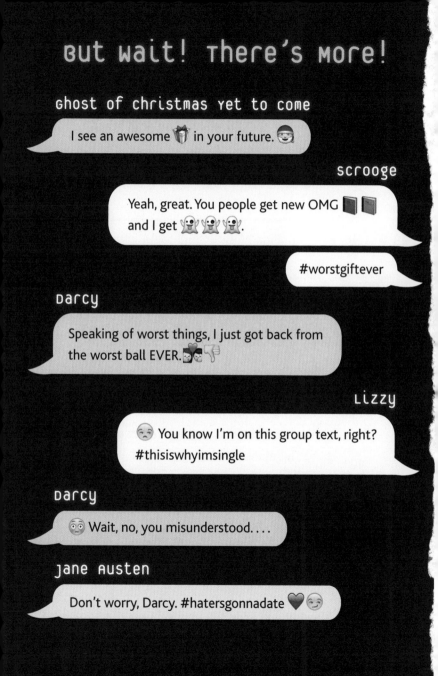